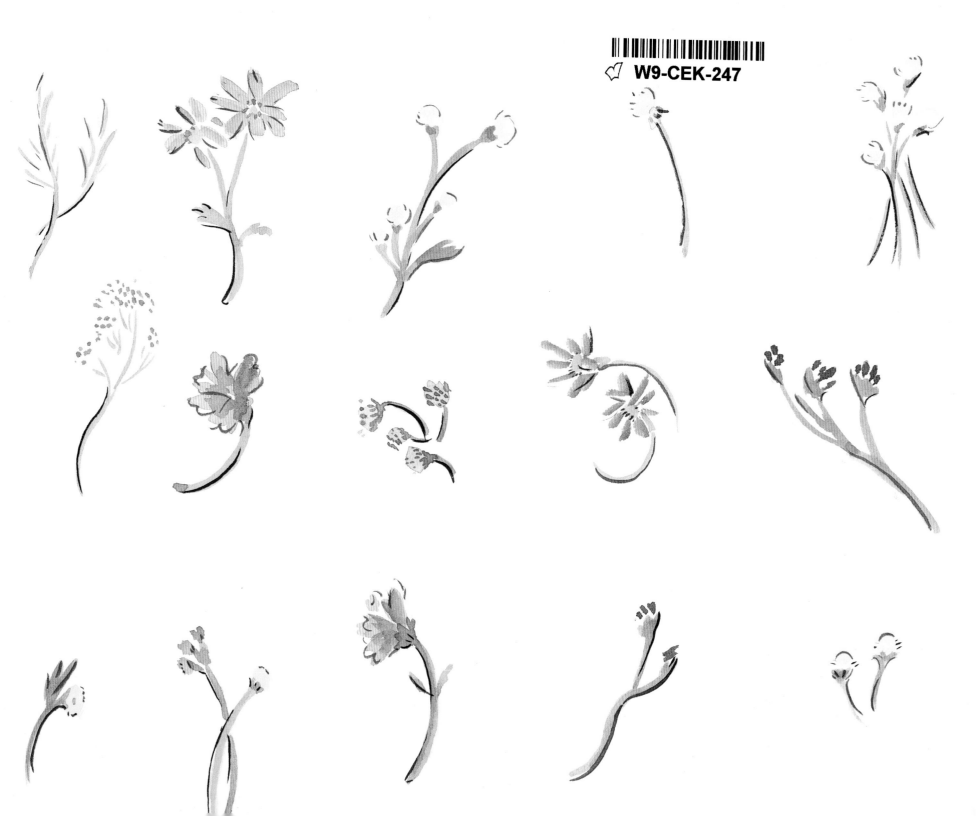

# Love, Sophia on the moon

BY Anica Mrose Rissi

ILLUSTRATED BY Mika Song

𝕯𝖎𝖘𝖓𝖊𝖞 • HYPERION

LOS ANGELES    NEW YORK

First Edition, March 2020
10 9 8 7 6 5 4 3 2 1
FAC-029191-20045
Printed in Malaysia
This book is hand lettered by Mika Song, with additional type in
Garamond MT Pro/Monotype.
Library of Congress Control Number: 2019945145

ISBN 978-1-368-02285-9
Reinforced binding
Visit www.DisneyBooks.com

For Sophia and her mother—A.M.R.

To Valerie and her Lola G.—M.S.

Dear Sophia,

Good news: I found someone nice to sleep in your bed. His name is Grorg and he came here from the moon. He says he ran away and is never going back, because the man on the moon was so mean. I've invited him to stay with me.

What should I make for dinner? I bet he'd like spaghetti. I'm glad you are having so much fun.

Love, Mom

Dear mom,
Moon kids are all very allergic to spaghetti. You should serve Grorg mud pies and old, soggy spinach instead.
We are having starlight soup with moonberry tarts, and Frurgbert made asteroid tea. After dinner he will teach us how to moonwalk.
Mr. Wubbles says hello and don't worry, he's not homesick. There's still lots for us to do on the moon.
Love, Sophia

Dear Sophia,
Grorg likes that idea. So do I. See you at the landing pad at half past a comet?
Love,
Mom

Dear mom,
Mr. Wubbles says he thinks Grorg might secretly be moonsick. maybe you should send him home. I bet the man on the moon would be happy to see him. You could come here too, if you want.
Love, Sophia

Dear Mom,
when you come to the moon, could you please bring Soft Blankie? Mr. Wubbles forgot to pack it. Love,
Sophia

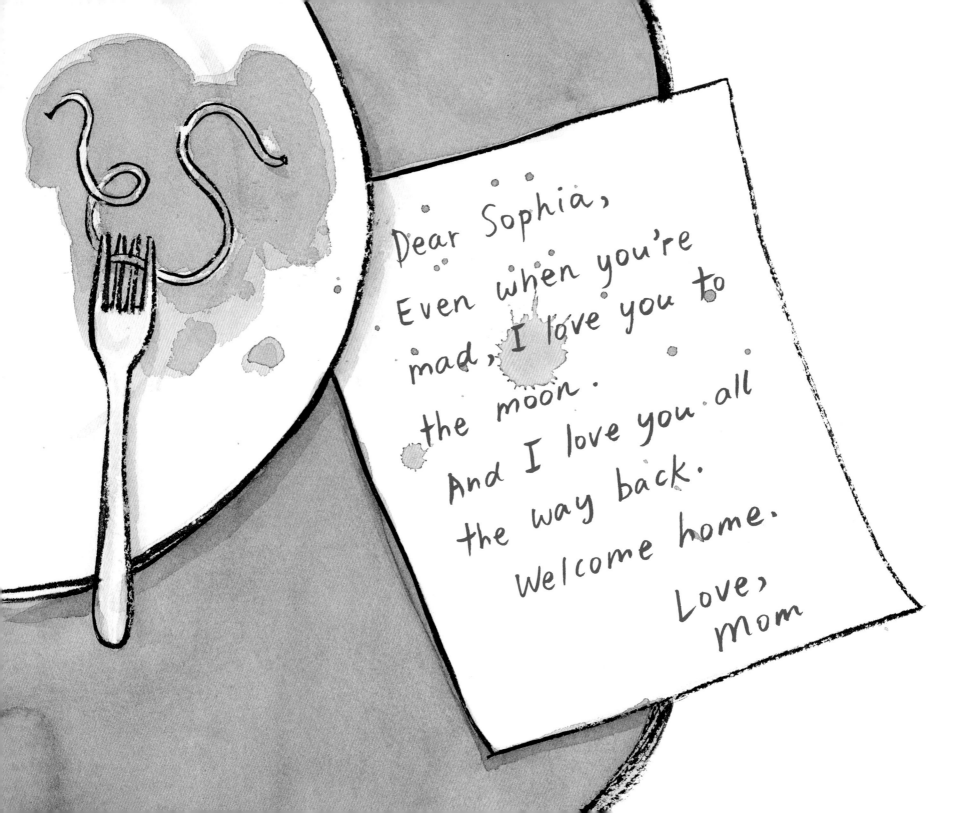